Arrorró, Mi Niño

Latino Lullabies and Gentle Games

Selected and Illustrated by
Lulu Delacre

MUSICAL ARRANGEMENTS BY
CECILIA ESQUIVEL
AND DIANA SÁEZ

LEE & LOW BOOKS INC. • NEW YORK

PARA TODAS LAS LATINAS QUE CRÍAN A SUS NIÑOS
EN LOS ESTADOS UNIDOS DE AMÉRICA—L.D.

Manufactured in China

Book design by Tania Garcia
Book production by The Kids at Our House

The text is set in Weiss
The illustrations are rendered in oil washes
  on primed Bristol board

HC 10 9 8 7 6 5 4
PB 10 9 8 7 6 5 4 3 2 1
First Edition

Library of Congress Cataloging-in-Publication Data
Arrorró mi niño : Latino lullabies and gentle games /
selected and illustrated by Lulu Delacre.— 1st ed.
  p. cm.
English and Spanish.
Summary: An illustrated collection of nursery rhymes,
finger play games, and lullabies from the major Latino
groups living in the United States today.
ISBN 978-1-58430-159-2 (hc) ISBN 978-1-60060-441-6 (pb)
1. Nursery rhymes, Spanish American. 2. Lullabies,
Spanish—Texts. 3. Children's songs—Latin America—Texts.
[1. Nursery rhymes. 2. Finger play. 3. Lullabies. 4. Spanish
language materials—Bilingual.] I. Delacre, Lulu.
PZ74.3.A77 2004   2003009234

Todavía recuerdo la primera vez que tomé a mi hija mayor en brazos para arrullarla. Al acunarla, una tierna canción emergió de entre los más recónditos rincones de mi memoria, como si hubiese estado esperando con paciencia el llamado de los tenues gemidos de mi bebé. Luego descubrí que era esa la misma nana que mi madre me cantaba en Puerto Rico cuando yo era niña.

Estas primeras canciones ayudan a crear fuertes lazos entre padres e hijos. En el momento en que una madre suscita gorjeos de alegría en su pequeño al cantar o jugar con él, nada más parecería importar, ambos encantados con el deleite de estar juntos. ¿Qué podría brindar mayor bienestar al bebé que el que un adulto amorosamente lo tome en su regazo y le cante?

En mis años de residencia en los Estados Unidos he conocido incontables mujeres latinas de todos los niveles socioeconómicos, cuyos hijos, al igual que mis hijas, aprenden a amar dos culturas y dos lenguas al criarse aquí. Las quince selecciones de versos en este libro han sido compiladas a partir de las remembranzas de muchas de estas mujeres latinas, provenientes de catorce países diferentes. Estas nanas y juegos sencillos han sobrevivido el transcurso del tiempo y el viaje entre países. Están ahora aquí reunidos para ayudarle a disfrutar de este bello folclor al jugar con su bebé, o al arrullarlo antes de dormir.

I still remember the first time I held my older daughter in my arms to lull her to sleep. As I held her, a soothing song surfaced from deep within my memory, as if it had been waiting to be called upon by the soft cries of my baby. I later found out that this song was the same lullaby my mother had sung to me as a child in Puerto Rico.

These first songs help create a strong bond between parent and child. The instant a mother plays with or sings to her baby and elicits laughter, nothing else seems to matter. The two of them are wrapped in the joy of being together. What could be more comforting to your baby than being held, cuddled, and sung to by a loving adult?

During my years living in the United States, I have met countless Latinas from all walks of life whose children grow up as mine do, learning and loving two cultures and two languages. The fifteen selections in this book were compiled from the recollections of many of those Latinas, originally from fourteen different countries. These sweet lullabies and gentle games have withstood the test of time and travel across nations. They are now gathered in this book to help you rejoice in this beautiful lore as you play with your baby or cuddle just before bedtime.

—L.D.

arrorró (ah-rroh-RROH): a soothing, lilting
Spanish word used to lull a baby to sleep

TORTITA

Tortita, tortita,
tortita de casabe,
para mamá
que bien lo sabe.

Tortita, tortita,
tortita de maíz tostado,
para papá
que está enojado.

*Enséñale a tu niño a aplaudir
al compás del poema.*

PAT-A-CAKE

Pat-a-cake, pat-a-cake,
round little fish cake,
for Mama
who knows all well.

Pat-a-cake, pat-a-cake,
round toasted corn cake,
for Papa
who is unhappy.

*Show your child how to clap hands
to the rhythm of the chant.*

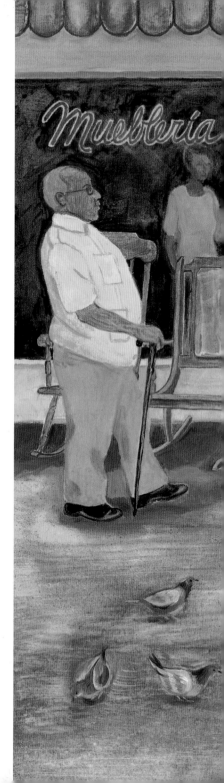

PON, PON, PON

Pon, pon, pon
el dedito en el pilón.

*Enséñale a tu niño a dar golpecitos
con el índice de una mano en la
palma de la otra al compás del poema.*

PUT, PUT, PUT

Put, put, put
your little finger in the cup.

*Show your child how to tap the cupped
palm of one hand with the index finger
of the other to the rhythm of the chant.*

Un huevito

Este dedito compró un huevito,
éste lo puso a hacer,
éste le echó la sal,
éste lo probó
y este pícaro gordo
¡se lo comió!

*Cierra en un puño la mano de tu niño. Comienza
por el meñique a abrir uno a uno los dedos con cada
verso. Termina por hacerle cosquillas bajo el brazo.*

A little egg

This little finger bought a little egg,
this one decided to cook it,
this one sprinkled it with salt,
this one tasted it,
and this naughty chubby one
gobbled it up!

*Have your child make a fist. Starting with the
little finger, lift a finger as you say each line.
With the last line, tickle your child under the arm.*

AL MERCADO

Cuando vayas al mercado,
no compres carne ni de aquí,
ni de aquí,
ni de aquí,
solamente ¡de por aquí!

*Extiende el brazo de tu niño y dale un toque
en la muñeca. Con cada verso sigue dando
toques brazo arriba. Termina por hacerle
cosquillas bajo el brazo.*

TO MARKET

When going to market,
do not buy meat from here,
nor here,
nor here.
Only buy it from over here!

*Hold your child's arm outstretched and tap
the wrist. As you say each line, tap a spot
farther up the arm. With the last line, tickle
your child under the arm.*

LA HORMIGUITA

Sube, sube la hormiguita,
sube, sube ¡por la montañita!

*Extiende el brazo de tu niño y a partir de
su muñeca, camina tus dedos lentamente
brazo arriba. Termina por hacerle
cosquillas bajo el brazo.*

THE TINY ANT

Up it climbs, up it climbs,
   an ant so tiny,
up it climbs, up it climbs
   the mountain mighty!

*Hold your child's arm outstretched. Starting at
the hand, slowly walk your fingers up to the
shoulder. Then tickle your child under the arm.*

Cinco pollitos

Cinco pollitos
tiene mi tía.
Uno le canta,
otro le pía
y otros le tocan
la sinfonía.

Toma la mano abierta de tu niño.
Ciérrale el pulgar, seguido del índice,
según indican los versos. Con el
verso final cierra los dedos restantes.

Five baby chicks

My auntie owns
five baby chicks.
One sings for her,
another one cheeps,
and three others play
a grand symphony.

Take your child's open hand. Fold
the thumb and then the index finger
toward the palm. With the last line,
fold the last three fingers all at once.

¡ARRE, CABALLITO!

¡Arre, caballito!
Vamos a Belén,
que mañana es fiesta
y pasa'o también.

*Mueve tus piernas al compás del poema para
que tu niño dé saltitos sentado en tu regazo.*

HURRY, LITTLE PONY!

Hurry, little pony!
Let's ride to Bethlehem.
Tomorrow is a holiday
and so is the next day.

*With your child on your lap, bounce your
legs up and down to the rhythm of the chant.*

SANA, SANA

Sana, sana,
colita de rana.
Si no sanas hoy,
sanarás mañana.

*Usa estas palabras maravillosas para
consolar a tu niño luego de una caída.*

THERE, THERE

There, there,
little frog's tail.
If today you don't heal,
tomorrow you will.

*Use these special words to comfort
and soothe your child after a fall.*

LOS POLLITOS

Los pollitos dicen
pío, pío, pío,
cuando tienen hambre,
cuando tienen frío.

La mamá les busca
el maíz y el trigo,
les da la comida
y les presta abrigo.

Bajo sus dos alas,
acurrucaditos,
hasta el otro día,
duermen los pollitos.

FLUFFY CHICKS

Fluffy chicks like singing
cheep, cheep, cheep,
whenever they feel hungry,
whenever they feel chilly.

Mama hen now brings them
wheat and golden corn,
feeds them tasty dinners,
blankets them with feathers.

Huddled all together
under her two wings
till the break of dawn,
the fluffy chicks will dream.

Pimpón

Pimpón es un muñeco
muy grande y de cartón,
se lava la carita
con agua y con jabón.

Se desenreda el pelo
con peine de marfil,
y aunque se da jalones
no llora ni hace ji.

Cuando las estrellitas
comienzan a salir,
Pimpón se va a la cama,
se acuesta y a dormir.

Pimpon

Pimpon is a big doll,
a made-of-cardboard doll.
His face he gently washes
with water and with soap.

His messy hair he brushes
with an ivory comb,
and should he pull a strand
he neither cries nor peeps.

As soon as up above
the stars begin to show,
Pimpon goes straight to bed
to snuggle in and sleep.

Luna, lunera

Luna, lunera,
cascabelera,
ojos azules,
cara morena.

Moon, gentle moon

Moon, gentle moon,
jingle-bell moon,
sky-lit blue eyes,
amber-faced moon.

ARRORRÓ, MI NIÑO

Arrorró, mi niño,
arrorró, mi sol,
arrorró, pedazo
de mi corazón.

Este niño lindo
se quiere dormir
y el pícaro sueño
no quiere venir.

Arrorró, mi niño,
arrorró, mi sol,
arrorró, pedazo
de mi corazón.

HUSH-A-BYE, MY CHILD

Hush-a-bye, my child,
hush-a-bye, my sun,
hush-a-bye, tiny piece
of my very own.

This beloved child
yearns to fall asleep,
but the naughty sandman
has yet to bring sweet dreams.

Hush-a-bye, my child,
hush-a-bye, my sun,
hush-a-bye, tiny piece
of my very own.

Esta niña linda

Esta niña linda
no quiere dormir,
cierra los ojitos
y los vuelve a abrir.

Duérmete mi niña,
carita de luz.
El mundo es tu cuna,
cuando duermes tú.

This beautiful girl

This beautiful girl
will not fall asleep,
closes both her eyes
but opens them to peek.

Sleep, beautiful girl,
face full of bright light.
The world is your cradle
when you sleep at night.

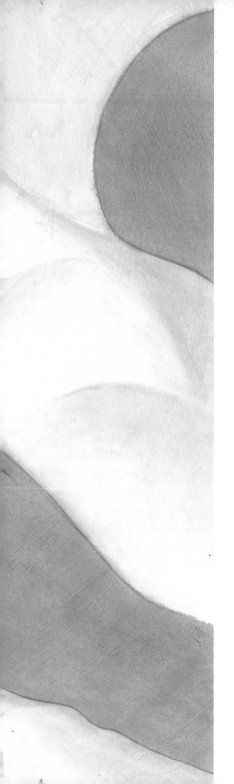

Este niño lindo

Este niño lindo
por fin se durmió,
que lo cuide el ángel
que le manda Dios.

This darling baby boy

This darling baby boy
is finally asleep.
May his guardian angel
come watch over him.

LINDOS ANGELITOS

Lindos angelitos,
abejas de luz,
cuidan mi tesoro,
en la noche azul.

LOVELY LITTLE ANGELS

Lovely little angels,
buzzing bees of light,
watch over my treasure
in the deep blue night.

A no todas las selecciones en este libro se les conoce melodía. "Un huevito", "Al mercado" y "La hormiguita" se pueden recitar rítmicamente. Una voz dulce para "Sana, sana" sería lo preciso.

Not all selections in this book have known melodies. "A Little Egg," "To Market," and "The Tiny Ant" may be recited in a sing-song voice. For "There, There," a soothing voice will be just right.

TORTITA

Tor - ti - ta, tor - ti - ta, tor - ti - ta de ca -
sa - be, pa - ra ma - má que bien lo sa - be. Tor -
ti - ta, tor - ti - ta, tor - ti - ta de ma - íz tos -
ta - do, pa - ra pa - pá que_es - tá_e - no - ja - do.

PAT-A-CAKE

Pat-a-cake, pat-a-cake,
round little fish cake,
for Mama
who knows all well.

Pat-a-cake, pat-a-cake,
round toasted corn cake,
for Papa
who is unhappy.

PON, PON, PON

Pon, pon, pon el de - di - to_en el pi - lón.

PUT, PUT, PUT

Put, put, put
your little finger in the cup.

Cinco pollitos

Cin-co po-lli-tos tie-ne mi tí-a. U-no le can-ta,

o-tro le pí-a y_o-tros le to-can la sin-fo-ní-a.

FIVE BABY CHICKS

*My auntie owns
five baby chicks.
One sings for her,
another one cheeps,
and three others play
a grand symphony.*

¡Arre, caballito!

¡A-rre, ca-ba-lli-to! Va-mos a Be-lén,

que ma-ña-na_es fies-ta y pa-sa'o tam-bién.

HURRY, LITTLE PONY!

*Hurry, little pony!
Let's ride to Bethlehem.
Tomorrow is a holiday
and so is the next day.*

Los pollitos

Los po-lli-tos di-cen pí-o, pí-o, pí-o,
La ma-má les bus-ca el ma-íz y_el tri-go,
Ba-jo sus dos a-las, a-cu-rru-ca-di-tos,

cuan-do tie-nen ham-bre, cuan-do tie-nen frí-o.
les da la co-mi-da y les pres-ta_a bri-go.
has-ta_el o-tro dí-a, duer-men los po-lli-tos.

FLUFFY CHICKS

*Fluffy chicks like singing
cheep, cheep, cheep,
whenever they feel hungry,
whenever they feel chilly.*

*Mama hen now brings them
wheat and golden corn,
feeds them tasty dinners,
blankets them with feathers.*

*Huddled all together
under her two wings
till the break of dawn,
the fluffy chicks will dream.*

Pimpón

Pim - pón es un mu - ñe - co muy gran-de_y de car - tón, se
Se de-sen-re-da_el pe - lo con pei - ne de mar - fil, y_aun-
Cuan - do las es-tre - lli - tas co - mien-zan a sa - lir, Pim -

la - va la ca - ri - ta con a - gua_y con ja - bón.
que se da ja - lo - nes no llo - ra ni_ha - ce ji.
pón se va_a la ca - ma, se_a - cues - ta y_a dor - mir.

PIMPON

Pimpon is a big doll,
a made-of-cardboard doll.
His face he gently washes
with water and with soap.

His messy hair he brushes
with an ivory comb,
and should he pull a strand
he neither cries nor peeps.

As soon as up above
the stars begin to show,
Pimpon goes straight to bed
to snuggle in and sleep.

Luna, Lunera

Lu - na, lu - ne - ra, cas - ca - be - le - ra,

o - jos a - zu - les, ca - ra mo - re - na.

MOON, GENTLE MOON

Moon, gentle moon,
jingle-bell moon,
sky-lit blue eyes,
amber-faced moon.

Arrorró, mi niño

A-rro-rró, mi ni-ño, a-rro-rró, mi sol, a-rro-rró, pe-da-zo de mi co-ra-zón. Es-te ni-ño lin-do se quie-re dor-mir y_el pí-ca-ro sue-ño no quie-re ve-nir. A-rro-rró, mi ni-ño, a-rro-rró, mi sol, a-rro-rró, pe-da-zo de mi co-ra-zón.

HUSH-A-BYE, MY CHILD

Hush-a-bye, my child,
hush-a-bye, my sun,
hush-a-bye, tiny piece
of my very own.

This beloved child
yearns to fall asleep,
but the naughty sandman
has yet to bring sweet dreams.

Hush-a-bye, my child,
hush-a-bye, my sun,
hush-a-bye, tiny piece
of my very own.

Esta niña linda

Es-ta ni-ña lin-da no quie-re dor-mir,
Duér-me-te mi ni-ña, ca-ri-ta de luz.
cie-rra los o-ji-tos y los vuel-ve_a abrir.
El mun-do_es tu cu-na, cuan-do duer-mes tú.

THIS BEAUTIFUL GIRL

This beautiful girl
will not fall asleep,
closes both her eyes
but opens them to peek.

Sleep, beautiful girl,
face full of bright light.
The world is your cradle
when you sleep at night.

Este niño lindo

Es - te ni - ño lin - do   por fin se dur - mió,

que lo cui - de_el án - gel   que le man - da Dios.

THIS DARLING BABY BOY

This darling baby boy
is finally asleep.
May his guardian angel
come watch over him.

Lindos angelitos

Lin - dos an - ge - li - tos,   a - be - jas de luz,

cui - dan mi te - so - ro,   en la no - che_a zul.

LOVELY LITTLE ANGELS

Lovely little angels,
buzzing bees of light,
watch over my treasure
in the deep blue night.

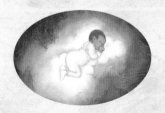